Dear Parent:

Congratulations! Your child is taking the first steps on an exciting journey. The destination? Independent reading!

STEP INTO READING® will help your child get there. The program offers books at five levels that accompany children from their first attempts at reading to reading success. Each step includes fun stories, fiction and nonfiction, and colorful art. There are also Step into Reading Sticker Books, Step into Reading Math Readers, and Step into Reading Phonics Readers— a complete literacy program with something to interest every child.

Learning to Read, Step by Step!

Ready to Read   Preschool–Kindergarten
• big type and easy words • rhyme and rhythm • picture clues
For children who know the alphabet and are eager to begin reading.

Reading with Help   Preschool–Grade 1
• basic vocabulary • short sentences • simple stories
For children who recognize familiar words and sound out new words with help.

Reading on Your Own   Grades 1–3
• engaging characters • easy-to-follow plots • popular topics
For children who are ready to read on their own.

Reading Paragraphs   Grades 2–3
• challenging vocabulary • short paragraphs • exciting stories
For newly independent readers who read simple sentences with confidence.

Ready for Chapters   Grades 2–4
• chapters • longer paragraphs • full-color art
For children who want to take the plunge into chapter books but still like colorful pictures.

STEP INTO READING® is designed to give every child a successful reading experience. The grade levels are only guides. Children can progress through the steps at their own speed, developing confidence in their reading, no matter what their grade.

Remember, a lifetime love of reading starts with a single step!

www.stepintoreading.com

Educators and librarians, for a variety of teaching tools, visit us at
www.randomhouse.com/teachers

Library of Congress Cataloging-in-Publication Data
Gaines, Isabel.
  Pooh's Christmas sled ride / Isabel Gaines ; illustrated by Studio
Orlando. —1st Random House ed.
    p. cm. — (Step into reading. A step 1 book)
"Based on the 'Winnie the Pooh' works by A. A. Milne and E. H. Shepard."
SUMMARY: Piglet keeps falling off the sled before the friends from the
Hundred Acre Wood even start down the big hill, and they try various
ways to keep him aboard before finding one that works.
ISBN 0-7364-2165-3 (trade)—ISBN 0-7364-8024-2 (lib. bdg.)
  [1. Sledding—Fiction. 2. Pigs—Fiction. 3. Toys—Fiction.
4. Animals—Fiction.] I. Milne, A. A. (Alan Alexander), 1882–1956.
II. Studio Orlando. III. Title. IV. Series: Step into reading. Step 1 book.
  PZ7.G1277Poe 2003 [E]—dc21 2003000382

Printed in the United States of America   10 9 8 7 6   5 4 3 2

Disney

Pooh's Christmas Sled Ride

By Isabel Gaines

Illustrated by Studio Orlando

Random House 🏠 New York

Pooh wakes up.

He wants to
go sledding!

Pooh goes to
Owl's house.

Owl wants to
go sledding, too.

Everyone will sled
down the big hill!

Down, down, down
they go!

"Whee!"

Hang on, Piglet!

Oh, dear!

Piglet falls off.

Where is Piglet?

Everyone goes
back up the hill.

There is Piglet!

Piglet sits up high.
Down, down, down
they go!

Oh, no!

Piglet falls off again.

Where is Piglet?

Everyone goes
back up the hill.

There is Piglet!
"Ride in front
with Roo,"
says Pooh.

Piglet rides in front.

Down, down, down
they go.
Oh, my!
Piglet falls off.

Where is Piglet?

There he is—
still up, up, up
the hill!

"Next time we
will hold you!"
says Christopher Robin.

Christopher Robin
holds Piglet tight.

Then everyone
holds Piglet tight.
Piglet stays put!

Down, down, down
they go!
Everyone has fun—
Piglet most of all!